AMORPHOUS TIDES

A FANTASY NOVELETTE

ANTONIO ROBERTS

Copyright © August 2021, first edition, by Antonio N. Roberts

ISBN 978-1-95-8664-00-1 eBook

ISBN 978-1-95-8664-01-8 Paperback

theantonioroberts.com

❀ Created with Vellum

To the Active Alumni and Mustache Cartel

-For keeping me writing

AMORPHOUS TIDES

*D*arla's host had swapped bodies three times before the age of thirty, and that wasn't the worst part.

Her host, dubbed "Dylan Wexwood"—not by birth—dressed as an unassuming businessman with a thick beard, rich dark skin, and stunning brown irises. At least Darla thought they were stunning. She, much like he, had grown to adore make-believe, pretending to be somebody else. The idea enraptured her—this metamorphosis, this unraveling of skin and peeling of flesh to uncover the burgundy pulp inside. After all, it was the heart that truly mattered. Darla desired—no, needed—a change. She *must* have it.

It had been too long since their last swap. Like any relationship, theirs required work. Between feeding a premature eldritch kindergartener and dodging assassins as an undead outlaw, breathing and safety proved a luxury. That's where swaps came in.

During a swap, Dylan parted ways with one body, breathing his living soul into a dead corpse, and Darla scurrying her teensy pink suckers into a new skull for her to grow. Not only did Darla exchange bodies, but Dylan as well through her dark powers.

Of course, they never took a life. Darla knew better. The last "accident" had ended her in a four-day time-out, and Darla couldn't bear the silent treatment.

Darla drummed her stubby suckers. She hated to consider the toll her magic took on her host. But he'd never leave her. It baffled her. Why? And were they finding bodies more frequently now? At least the city catered to one of their needs.

In Narcopolis, the city of the dead, nothing ever went to waste if one knew where to look or greased a palm in silver. Everyone had to take risks once in a while according to Dylan.

Body transfers or swapping proved only another leg up in survival, especially in a city of assassins and violence. With a price on their heads and health, their last swap had been pivotal.

Darla wondered, *how long had it been?*

Truthfully, neither of them could remember when exactly it had happened. Memories crinkled easily between transfers, cheap tissue paper things. It was a wonder that bodies held together at all, exerting one slimy, wet soul into a fresh tank. Not the prettiest of magic, but it was life.

Of recent, Darla found herself like a bored housewife, turning and chewing at scrumptious memories of his hippocampus. Being a juvenile rakehell squid meant Darla's life demanded two things: a warm body and entertainment.

This morning favored the latter. Darla slithered inside Dylan's skull restlessly until he shuddered.

He flicked the back of his neck. *Stop that,* he thought.

Darla sighed, wishing he could see her luminescent fish-eye roll. She crossed her slimy appendages, drumming her suckers in a pout. Dylan never let her have any fun.

Five more minutes, please, he thought.

Darla exhaled and extended an arm down his optic nerve. At least if she was bored she could look out a window during her ride.

Darla's eye scrunched shut as she tapped his sight from his spinal cord.

In the open, dry heat, Dylan combed the Narcopolis bazaar. Hundreds of desert tents flapped, whipping in the breeze. The acrid stench of fresh two-headed trout bit his nose and throat as neon lights glinted above them, humming in the dim shadow of sandstone skyscrapers.

As they ambled along, the bazaar streets grew louder. Midday criers preached the good news. Gossip spilled like blood, trickling thick and juicy, and spurted into the raucous menageries of men chattering business. Oh, the babble of it all.

Darla withdrew her tentacles to breathe and shuddered. That racket she could have done without. She couldn't hear herself think, let alone her host.

Of course, being born premature hadn't helped Darla either. She relied on his lungs, his sustenance, and his senses as hers developed. But as Dylan's vigor drained, so did Darla's. Perhaps this body had grown old on her and Dylan—her Dylan.

Her insides warmed with pride at the thought of her adopted father and friend. Dylan had proved more than a host but also a hefty burden on her heart. She found herself proud to call him her own. If any meat sack so much as dared think little of him, she'd probe their brains from their eye sockets until they popped. No one messed with her daddy.

Puddles splashed from last night's rain under Dylan's sandals, and damp cloth canopied the dingy stalls.

"Daddy, where are we going?" probed Darla. Ever innocent, she'd caused him to accidentally speak aloud. She had forgotten to detach from his motor functions.

The tired father took a deep breath. "We are looking for work, dear."

"Again?" Darla said, craning her host's neck. "I thought we'd given up on that. You, me, and nothing but wet work caravans through the magic-infested bush. We had a plan."

Dylan shook his head, trying to maintain control of his own body. "Plans change."

"Since when?" rattled Darla. "We're a team. I napped for five minutes, and you have already changed your mind? What about us?"

Passersby threw strange glances at the man arguing with himself.

Dylan raised the straw hat that dangled from his shoulders. Bowing his head, he ignored Darla's questions, internally pleading she keep a lower profile.

Sadly, like any dutiful daughter, Darla had to know everything about anything. This silent treatment would not do. He'd asked for it.

Darla lurched, anchoring her grip into his motor functions, until Dylan collapsed, holding his gut.

"Daddy, do you hear me?" she roared. "I asked you a question!"

Narcopolis pedestrians stopped and stared but, nonetheless, funneled around, keeping their distance or calmly turning the other way. No one dared address the lunatic in the street.

Dylan's eyes watered. "Yes, I hear you. I . . . I haven't felt good."

Darla's teensy beak puckered in sympathy before calmly releasing her grip over his body.

She hadn't realized it until now, but his toe nerves had felt supple today. Dylan must have the urge to swap hosts, too, she thought. Darla cuttlefish-kissed his brain and tugged his arms like an amateur puppeteer.

"I'll drive."

Dylan slapped himself. "Oh, no, you don't. Last time you nearly got us killed."

Darla whined. "Aw, but Daddy, I'm bored."

"Use your imagination."

Dylan's arms crossed against his will until he regained his senses.

"But I already did that," she argued, "and you won't let me eat yours . . . anymore."

"Darla, we need stable work," he spoke firmly. "The city thieves' guild will find us again, and when they do, I need money to protect us. Freelance doctoring is great, but we need something stable. Also low-profile."

"Daddy, you're much too paranoid," Darla replied matter-of-factly. "Please let me drive. Pretty please. I promise not to take us swimming this time."

Dylan dusted himself off. "No. I'm not plucking goose-badger feathers from my teeth again," he said.

Darla gasped at the notion. "They were swan-monkeys and you know it!"

Dylan put his foot down. "Whatever. We're finding work, and that's final."

Darla balled her tentacles into tiny fists. "You never let me have any fun," she muttered.

Dylan checked over his shoulder as bazaar police approached. Steel breastplates caged their chests, dyed leather trousers provided more padding than protection, and their skull-shaped helmets shrouded their faces in a ghoulish countenance, matching their namesake, the Undying Watch.

Dylan put his head down, disappearing into the crowd. "Can it," he hushed. "You're making a scene."

Darla squirted a raspberry in cute defiance. Darn her

stubby tentacles! Had she the size, she'd rule this city, bring it to its knees, and force all the fleshy humans to feed her cookies and those scrumdiddlyumptious childhood memories. No one would stand against her—no, not one. No one could tell her no, or say, "Stop eating that," "Don't put that in your mouth," or impose bedtimes. Never. Sleep was for the weak. When she ruled the world, bedtimes would be the first to go. *None shall be spared, save maybe Daddy, as he is old anyway,* she thought.

Darla bubbled in her scheming. *Yes, all shall quake, tremble.* All would perish beneath her mighty pink suction cups as she drew her minions wretched scribbles in magic marker. Aggressive scribbles meant business. Every eldritch horror knew that.

Darla exhaled, perching herself loftily atop her cranium throne, and glanced around her empty skull. Finally, she shrank, bored and trapped yet again. Ever so gingerly, she crept a tentacle to peer through the window to the outside world once more.

Dylan tested the quality of rugs while window-shopping.

You know we lost our apartment, Darla reminded telepathically.

Dylan rubbed his temples. His ten minutes of peace were gone.

Darla nudged further. *We lost it when our friends abandoned us, remember? We're alone.*

Nodding, Dylan set the rug down and kept walking.

Do you even have any idea for a job? she asked.

Dylan rubbed his chin, weighing the question. "I'll know it when we find it," he said aloud.

And if we don't?

Then we take the caravans, he replied telepathically. *Preferably after swapping skins again, so the assassins can't track us.*

Darla leaped with joy. *Oh, I'd love a new body, Daddy! Can our next one have blue eyes? When's the next swap?*

Only if we fail, he warned. *Job hunt first.*

Darla replied without missing a beat. *Right. Sabotage the interviews. Got it.*

Dylan's eyes bucked. "No! You will do no such thing. Promise you'll be a good little parasite," he declared aloud.

A grubby vagrant boy froze and slowly placed his stolen apple back as the previously oblivious merchant gaped at Dylan.

Dylan shot through the streaming crowds and found a bench.

Darla giggled in mischief.

Not as amused, Dylan cleared his throat. He used his grown-up voice again. "Darla."

Inside the skull, Darla raised her right stub. "Ahem. I, Darla, supreme empress of kindergarten, do solemnly swear not to sabotage any of Daddy's job hunts today."

Dylan nodded in approval.

"Even though he has gotten old, fat, his bones creak, and he probably has no prospects to speak of."

Dylan rolled his eyes. "Okay, that's enough."

"Also, your feet stink. A lot," she added. "We should probably wash those."

Dylan drummed his fingers against his cheek, keeping a lid on his temper.

"Thank you, Darla. I suppose your word will have to do."

With a smirk, Darla clicked her beak in chipper dolphin delight. She cut telepathic connection and raised her crossed tentacles from behind her back. An evil, maniacal laugh escaped her. *Mwah-ha-ha-ha-ha!* He had fallen for the oldest trick in the book: Never make a deal with a little girl unless you can see all five of her stubs.

Darla would enjoy this. She almost felt rotten lying to

Dylan, but with a new body at stake, she needed relief from her monotony. Dress-up was within her grasp; she could taste it.

Each failed interview proved too easy. During the fruit peddler's interview, Dylan developed a sudden course of sneezes over the produce. His arms grew slightly feebler at the steelworker's stall, and she didn't even have to sabotage the fish market. The smell did that for her. Things were going well.

Come noon, Dylan spent their remaining money on kabobs and naan. Their empty coin pouch folded flat and buffeted in the breeze, and without a penny to their name, Dylan determined to gather a second wind for both of them. Darla thumbed their brain for sustenance, daring him to bring it on.

Dylan bit a caramelized leek and chewed. "You know, you've been awfully quiet. Everything okay?" he asked.

Darla attached to the cerebrum to communicate. *Yup. Just enjoying the show,* she chimed.

Dylan guzzled his waterskin, finding less than expected. He sighed to himself. "I want you to know I'm trying. I'll take care of us. You'll see."

Darla nestled into his brain. Her plan had gone swimmingly. She would not only see but hold front-row seats.

Dylan leaned over an awning overlooking the canal. Choppy, stirring waves bucked beneath them, refracting glaring sunbeams.

Darla sensed him frown when she wished he hadn't. This body gave him a repulsive poopy face when he did.

How long till we face adventure? asked Darla.

"One more lap around the block. Then we hit the caravan as promised," he said, more to himself than her.

Darla smiled.

"You know, I'm proud of you," said Dylan.

Darla flushed peach. *Oh?*

"Yup. Not one interference in my interviews. You've really grown up, haven't you? Definitely not the same egg I saved from thieves, that's for sure."

Darla's squid heart panged.

"Just one more lap. Thanks for keeping your promise, dear. I'm glad I can trust you."

Darla detached rapidly. Was she shaking? Staring down at her stubs, she was sure she was. Guilt overwhelmed her body, and he couldn't know her thoughts.

She had lied, and he was proud of her? Her beak dried and her limbs curled. How could she live with herself?

From now on, no distractions or hijinks. Dylan would find a job without her hinderance, as promised. She only hoped it wasn't too late.

Alas, the next two vendors shot Dylan down as well, although not as easily. Darla assured him the men were just picky, and if she were a merchant, using her astute sense of taste, she'd hire her daddy in an instant. Dylan couldn't help but smile.

Stalls dwindled. Options grew thinner. He could search within the city limits again, but those jobs would be even harder, and as Darla had said, he had no prospects. What hope was there?

On his last stretch, a single stall caught his eye, bigger than all the rest. Its sign read, "Copernicus's Beauty Shop, Silk, and Sundries."

"That one," Dylan whispered.

Darla reached deeper into his sight to look.

A tailor? Daddy, we're criminal masterminds. We have no need for sewing. Sewing is beneath us. Have you ever heard of a supervillain with buttons?

No, really, thought Dylan. *Remember how we hemmed clothes*

and disguises in the guild before escaping? This is our chance. You know I always wanted—

To open your own beauty shop, I know, completed Darla with a groan. *I'm tired of hearing about it.*

A short, gnomish man exited the tent, laying fresh wares. With the sunset, he'd be taking in others. He sipped a glass of milk and appeared to choke before forcing it down.

Well, now's our chance, thought Dylan. He marched forward, leaving Darla to jostle atop his brain.

Wait! What are you doing? she cried.

Five minutes. Let me do the talking.

Darla buckled down and cringed. She couldn't bear to see him fail and wished nothing more than to leave. But if she interfered—no, Dylan had to trust her. Was her new body worth it?

Dylan acted first, approaching the tent of custom clothes. The shopkeeper appeared gnomish. Tinted luminescent skin and an ornate tunic covered his body, the latter hiding his squatty legs. He was so small that Dylan needed to crane over the counter to see him.

Finishing another glass of cream, the gnome jumped in surprise before bending to take a knee. "My, my, dear sir. You mustn't startle me this way," he cried.

Dylan rubbed his neck, worried he'd already blown his chances.

Darla tucked her beak and whispered words of encouragement. *You've got this, Daddy. Knock him dead. Metaphorically.*

"A thousand pardons, sir," said Dylan. "Are you all right?"

The gnome coughed, holding his chest. "Been better. Ouch. I'm afraid I must lie down. My slave can assist you." He wheezed and fumbled for a cane. "Giselle," his voice grated, hoarse. "Giselle! Come out here, you useless changeling."

A timid, blue, crane-faced woman with spectacles rising from her beak emerged from their tent. She rushed to usher her master inside and soothed his grumblings.

Dylan took a deep breath, thinking surely he'd blown it, until she appeared again. Their eyes locked, and her tame pupils blinked. The desert sunset lit her feathers as a fetching blossom. An alluring bronze bracelet with a shooting star charm burned brighter in the light, drawing Darla's eye. Had she seen this before?

Dylan's throat dried, and he retreated, facing away from the stall.

He whispered to Darla. "Psst!"

She attached eagerly. *I'm here Daddy.*

Did you see her?

Who?

The cute crane girl, he thought quietly.

Darla bent his neck to peek.

Dylan scolded, "Don't look!"

Hmm, she is quite pretty, isn't she? Yes, it's coming back to me. I ate a tasty memory of her once.

"Really?" Dylan said, astonished.

Absolutely, she replied. *Childhood, even.* Darla's mouth watered at the savory mention of more memories to consume.

Dylan broke a sweat.

Giselle neatly folded clothes in elegant motions and adjusted her glasses as they slid. Catching his view, she gave a perturbed wave, and Dylan flushed. He waved back, tongue-tied.

He raised a finger for one moment and whispered to Darla. "What do you think? Are you certain? Do we have a chance for a job here?"

One question at a time, Darla fussed. *She massaged his brain in thought and stopped. Daddy, your heart's beating faster. Are you all right?*

Dylan stole a glance at the radiant changeling as his heart fluttered. They both felt something they hadn't in quite some months.

"I did know her, Darla, and she's lovely. Why can't I recall?"

Darla stifled a laugh. *I'll say. Your brain and bloodstream are going ba-nay-nays. Something subconscious—affection, maybe? But I can't trace where. Your hormones are going haywire. I say it is best we head to the desert and regroup. Forget the job. Let's wrangle a new body and new names. What do you think? Daddy? Are you even listening?*

Dylan had lost himself in gazing at Giselle. Darla probed his thoughts, trying to dislodge him from Giselle-land, but it was no use.

He needed this job. If he took it, he might recall this maiden. If he took it, Darla could be fed and perhaps, if but for a short while, be safe.

Darla bit her host.

"Ouch, Darla!"

Dylan's whole left side sagged numb as she preached to him.

Did you not hear me? croaked Darla. *You're not thinking safe. Our body is failing us. We have two weeks tops. If we don't leave, we lose our chance at pinching a corpse from under the city's nose.*

Later, he replied. Dylan took a deep breath for courage and went in for the kill.

Inside, Darla steamed. Didn't he know this was suicide? He left her no choice but to sabotage this.

"Excuse me, miss," he called across the way.

Giselle's head perked. She tossed the fresh linens into a wicker basket. "We're closed," she said coldly, "no thanks to you."

"Yes, and I apologize. Let me help you. I can work the stall free of charge."

Like squid we are, spat Darla. *Are you seeking a job or not?*

Quiet, you, he thought.

The crane held out her hand. "Giselle."

Dylan reached to shake before Darla whipped his arm to slap it.

"Ow!" Giselle cried out.

Dylan leapt back. "Oh, I am so sorry," he said. "I don't know what came over me."

Giselle sucked on her palm, pushing him away. "What's wrong with you?"

"Muscle spasm. It was an accident, I swear. If you'd just let me . . ."

Giselle waved him off.

Inside the tent, Copernicus coughed in a fit and rasped for his servant.

"One moment," Giselle called. She adjusted her glasses to squint at Dylan. "You've helped enough. Why don't you hike back to wherever you came from?"

"I can't. Listen, I'm a doctor. If your hand is sprained or he's sick, I can take a look."

Giselle shook her head and glared at him in silence.

Darla popped her cups in a steeple formation. She was just getting started.

Giselle reluctantly handed her palm to Dylan, and Darla slithered to the olfactory sensors to give them a good rubbing.

According to plan, Dylan's nose twitched as he studied her soft, feathered palm. He spoke nasally. "The good news is it's not broken."

"Are you al—" Giselle began to ask before Dylan executed a nuclear snot blast, hosing his dear bird.

ANTONIO ROBERTS

Giselle wrenched away and wiped her face on the fresh linens.

Copernicus called again, "Giselle." His voice strained.

Dylan cringed, confused. "Miss, I am so sorry."

Giselle tossed the linen at him. "Take it and go. I have an old man to care for."

"Please, I need a job. I can help," he begged.

"You're disgusting and out of control. I don't want you here, and I'm sure my ailing master would feel the same."

Determined, Darla pulled out one final stop in her devious plot: flatulence. The fish market had stopped her from playing with her special toy earlier, and she relished whipping out the big guns. Darla determined she'd save them both. She extended a tentacle and plunged her suction cup over his stomach module, eager to fire when ready.

Outside, Dylan pleaded with Giselle. "Please. I know this seems bad, but this is my dream, and I have a daughter."

Darla froze.

"I don't always treat her the best, but she needs to be fed every day. Please, miss. I love her."

Darla looked down at her tentacles and dared to peer through the optic nerve. The scene shuttered and hazed with tears through her host's faltering eyes.

Giselle crossed her arms, shutting him out.

The damage had been done. The gun was cocked. Should Darla lift her sucker over his stomach functions, he'd let the unholiest of unholy ones rip, ruining any chances forever.

Dylan's eyes dripped, and he unknowingly wiped Darla's view free. She supposed Giselle was pretty. For a bird. It was difficult to tell with changelings. Mutant peoples held strange customs of beauty.

Had Giselle deserved this? Had Darla ruined this for Dylan?

Darla teetered aimlessly. There was no going back. Faced

with her final call, did she let it out quickly or strain his insides in hopes he could salvage this?

Dylan choked, "Giselle, I need to protect her."

Giselle shook her head and stepped backwards from the grotesque man.

Darla winced. Fearing it was too late, she took the plunge. They needed a new body.

Let me protect you, Darla whispered.

She raised her sucker, and Dylan's backend boomed into the stratosphere. A disgusting odor wrenched the air from his bowels, worsening the final situation of this urchin of a man.

Giselle gagged. She entered the tent without a final word to Dylan.

Defeated, he turned, heading to exit the city.

Darla remained silent yet alert. It had happened so fast she couldn't process what had transpired. She had won . . . hadn't she?

Dylan's dragging feet kicked up dust. Darla felt his throat dry and his stomach pinch like her own. He wiped his nose, and Darla eased control of an arm to fetch him a hankie.

Dylan nodded his thanks and kept his head down. The sun would set behind the city soon, and the guards shut the gates at night. If they didn't reach the caravan, it was trash bag pillows and cold concrete sheets again.

Their quiet walk unnerved Darla—the uneasiness, his prolonged breathing, and his heart beating in her ear. Darla hated the silence, yet she couldn't bring herself to speak. Had he found her out? Would he hate her?

Dylan skimmed his hand along an open stall as the crowds tumbled along. Balling his fist, he tossed it aside like his feelings. Discarded and unwanted. Was that all they were together? Darla wished to tap his thoughts but feared them and what she would learn.

The twilight breeze blew through his cloak, forcing a shiver from their frail, shared body.

Dylan exhaled, speaking low to Darla. "Do you remember the day we met?"

Her petite beak pursed. It was one of the few cherished memories she hadn't eaten. She had saved it for a rainy day, like a cherry tucked beneath the sofa cushions—a joyous snack too sweet to eat. She felt something . . . *strange* . . . whenever she'd find it.

Darla breathed, tapping his nerves. "Yes. Yes, I do. You found me atop the rubbish heap. We were kids then."

Dylan nodded.

"You fell from above and met my mother." Darla stopped. "What was left of her. . . . Did you ever meet her?"

Dylan weighed the question, floating his head from side to side. "Once," he said. "She kept you warm."

"She was cold when you found her," Darla added.

Dylan bit his lip. He said nothing.

"You had warm hands in that body," said Darla. "Fur too. Rich, fluffy fur, thick as elephant grass at night."

Dylan bit his cheek lazily, as if failing to recall.

"Daddy?"

"Yes, Darla?"

"Will we ever find a home?"

Dylan took a seat. "I don't know, dear."

Darla scrunched in dread. The guilt gripped hard at her insides. Could Dylan still love her if he knew? What if he found out?

"You won't put me back in a trash heap with Momma, will you?"

Dylan turned his head. "Darla, why would I?"

"Because maybe you don't want me anymore."

Dylan pouted. "Oh, sweet pea, no. Come here." Dylan tapped his cheek to summon her, but she retreated further into his skull. Bone surrounded her, trapped in a prison she'd made. Her hot breaths huffed back at her in hollow echoes.

Dylan tapped his cheek, urging her again. "Come. Let me look at you."

Darla leapt from his brain, ashamed, clinging to the skeletal walls. She ducked further away. How could he see her like this? After all she'd done. It was because of her that Dylan's life was failing. Because of *her* and her toll on him, they must wander, beg, and grovel for pennies while dodging past lives. He may not see it, but he never would. Not if she ate the thoughts first. He couldn't know what she knew.

Dylan exhaled. "Darla, never think you're worthless. Do not speak like that. You weren't the only discarded one that day. I didn't fall. Did I tell you?"

Darla stared at his scarred, pink walnut of a brain. She wished she had never hurt him. Would it have been better for him without her? Curse him and his old-people stories.

"I didn't fall into those sewers. I was pushed. My brothers wanted rid of me. I had dreams. I had ambitions. And mostly, I had our father. He favored me over them, and it destroyed their hearts."

Darla scampered down the skull wall towards his throat. Her tentacle brushed his catacombic nerves and drumming heart. It yearned, beating fainter, reminiscent of her mother's. Darla crawled no further.

"I spoke to your mother, Darla."

Darla swallowed.

Dylan's mouth dried. "Or, rather, she spoke to me. She nursed me and questioned my deepest desire, and do you know what I said?"

Darla leaned in, still silent.

"A friend."

Darla's pupil watered. She pieced together his meaning.

"She gave me you. Beyond all your promise and powers,

beyond fights to walk again and get revenge on my brothers, you answered my greatest wish."

Darla struggled to fight the leaking liquids from her face. She wished and begged internally for him to stop but said nothing. She wished to be strong. Protection was her duty, not his.

"I love you Darla," he admitted, rising to his feet.

Immediately, Darla sobbed. She couldn't fight it anymore. Heat flushed her pink cephalopod cheeks, and saltwater tears drenched his mind. She reclimbed the skull.

Dylan strolled as Darla sniffed in the dark.

She reached and touched him to speak. "I'm sorry," she finally choked.

Dylan shushed her. He combed his beard, urging her to come out. "Let me hold you."

"Daddy, no. I'm sorry no one took you in today."

Dylan's soles grew heavy, and he rested against a stall to rub his feet. His everything ached. Darla sensed it, even though he hated her to.

"It's okay, Darla. It's not your fault."

Darla shut her eye. Her suckers curled into herself, and the lump pummeled deeper into her stomach. She let go and fell again before she whimpered into his pillowy cerebrum.

"I wish it wasn't."

"It's all right. I knew," he consoled her.

Darla sniffed and wailed louder between the folds of his mind.

"It's okay. Let me hold you."

Darla dripped tears and reached to the crevice beneath his left eye.

Dylan lightly patted his cheeks again, and Darla emerged into the fading light, drawing crimson. Dylan shed tears unwillingly as the tea-saucer-sized squid quivered into his palm.

Darla gazed up at her bleeding father, fearing he planned to squish her. But Dylan did no such thing.

Reading *her* mind for a change, he spoke, "I still love you, my little wish."

Darla withdrew her gaze. Her body caught the waning neon lights flicking on inside the city. Her pink crown crinkled in satin creases to her gold pupil slit, an eerie phantom in pale starlight. Five pentapod arms bent as pinky toes. *Ugly and fat*, thought Darla.

Dylan poked her playfully, and as if by some amorphous magic, he cleared the air. With one look, he did not feel the same.

Darla lightly caressed and hugged his finger. Her Dylan cradled her body atop his shoulder, patting her close, blinking as the bleeding ceased.

Darla inhaled. He smelt of pine and last night's garbage. The rich clothes had been pretend, too, she supposed. Something else thrown away, like them, felt right somehow.

"We'll make it," said Dylan. "I promise."

Darla gazed up at him. "And if we don't?"

His aching back cracked. Dylan seemed to know the answer just as she did.

"We keep trying," he said. "Your mother promised great things for both of us. If my wish came true, won't hers too?"

Darla hummed in thought. She knew little of her species. Ancient peoples believed the rakehell squids birthed the stars. Did wishes like theirs really come true? Or was that only pretend?

Dylan checked the city lights. The sun had set. Narcopolis city gates would close before they reached them, and neither Dylan nor Darla would get their way tonight.

"Same alley tonight, Darla?"

Darla's cheeks raised. "You know it. I love you, Daddy."

Dylan patted her head.

"Even though your feet stink," she added.

Neon signs crackled in blinking beads advertising the Webdeb Wharf, casinos, and "nightclubs," places Dylan forbade Darla to ask about. It always puzzled her why.

Tents shut and glowed with vendors inside. Some traded spaces for the evening, braving the thief-ridden city against reason. Everyone had to take a few risks now and again, Dylan always said.

Darla craned her neck. Giselle the seamstress's olive tent glowed, casting bent shadows and low moans. Darla supposed it was time she took her own risk.

Dylan passed, and still Darla watched the tent. She tugged his collar.

"Daddy?" she asked.

Dylan looked, and Darla kneaded her father's shirt. "Do you mind if I drive this evening?"

"No tricks?" he asked.

Darla's squid eye shut. She held all arms where he could see them. "I, Darla, supreme keeper of crayons and doodles, do solemnly swear to not swim this evening."

Dylan smiled.

"Even though Daddy's fat body is naturally buoyant, squids are made for water, and clothes favor the weak."

Dylan's countenance lowered. Reluctantly, he conceded.

Darla squeezed into his nasal cavity and tore at his nostril hair. Dylan shuddered at the procedure until his daughter stilled. Darla seated herself in. The malign and worn cushion suited her now in a homey plush.

Dylan took a breath to compose himself. "We need a better way to do that."

Cracking her knuckles and neck, she took the reins and turned Dylan around.

Dylan raised an eyebrow. "Where are we going?"

"Making a dream come true."

20

"Darla, please," he argued.

"This isn't a trick. We can try again," she said. "Please? It'll be fun. We did things your way all day. Where's your sense of adventure?"

Darla creeped into his thoughts, whispering more pleading.

It can't get any worse, Dylan thought.

With that, Darla paraded his body with a bounce in his step.

Walk normal! barked Dylan in thought.

"Oh, but Daddy, this is more fun."

Darla twirled and skipped to the seamstress's tent, drawing strange looks from dwindling bazaar patrons.

Darla danced outside the tent. For once, she had her adventure. Her Daddy loved her, and she would show him. She would get him this job or they'd collapse trying.

Dylan swayed dizzily and reached in his consciousness to take a knee for them. Their body huffed.

Low moaning called within the tent.

Darla, not so fast. We need to breathe a bit, thought Dylan.

Darla giggled. "You're too old, Daddy. Running is much faster."

The crane changeling's shadow shot erect. "Who goes there?"

Dylan took a deep breath.

Darla barged into the tent, grazing Giselle's hand along the other side. Dylan staggered backwards into a cauldron of aromatic stew. Alongside him, the gnomish peddler wheezed on his back. The shattered milk glass lay beside him, its spilled contents curdled and black. Copernicus held his chest, letting loose a clamorous moan.

Dylan fell awkwardly, still out of breath himself.

Giselle's stance widened. Her shooting star bracelet jingled as she pointed a crooked finger at him. "You," she breathed. "Get out. Out! He wasn't like this until you showed up. I bet you brought the rancid milk."

Dylan stared up at her, hyperventilating. "Hi," he said, giving a limp wave.

"Who is it?" asked merchant Copernicus in a wheeze.

"No one," shot Giselle. "Just some slum-rat-nobody fancying himself a doctor."

Copernicus coughed. "Doctor?"

Immediately, Giselle's neck feathers coiled. "Oh no. No. You are not—"

"Bring him to me," Copernicus interrupted.

Dylan crawled towards him.

Copernicus's chest heaved up and down. His wide hips carried too much weight, and his crow-footed eyes divulged his age. His pupils glazed with cataracts that Dylan hadn't noticed before.

This wasn't regular poison. Especially if had been hidden it in milk. While milk would hide most poisons' chalky texture, any substance immediately lethal would curdle the cream. This poison was supernatural.

Above them, the tent lantern swung as the desert winds crashed in.

"Get away from him," Giselle ordered. "Poisoner!"

Copernicus put up a weak arm to silence her. "Enough."

Dylan gently helped the old gnome lower it to his side.

Copernicus coughed. "Boy, should you heal me, I can pay you."

Darla's heart leapt.

Dylan choked on his spit. "Money?"

"He will not." Giselle dropped to face Dylan, opposite Copernicus's legs. "Master, he does not know what he's doing. Just earlier he acted erratically, and I do not trust him. It's his fault you're—"

Copernicus wheezed and held his chest. "Giselle, it is not," he said over her. He turned to face Dylan. "We are desperate. I cannot afford to pay you much, but what I can spare, you shall have. Giselle said you wished to work, yes?"

Dylan nodded, and Giselle admonished, "He can't see you. In fact, he can hardly see past his hand since you jinxed him. I bet you slipped him the nerve agent in his milk this morning. You're one of those demons or shapeshifters, aren't you?" she accused.

Darla balled Dylan's fist, wishing to take her outside.

"Darla, heel," he said aloud.

Giselle placed her hands on her hips. "Name's Giselle, dipstick. And I'm not an animal to be spoken to that way," she huffed. "And if you think you can waltz in to finish him off, you're sorely mistaken."

Dylan ignored her.

Darla, can we heal him? he thought.

Darla hummed. "Check his ribs."

Dylan felt Copernicus's bloated chest, and Darla sensed the vibrations of the tiny man's body. His lymph nodes read easier than a human's.

"I'll need to step outside," said Darla aloud through Dylan.

"Like heck you do," snapped Giselle. "You've done enough."

"Peace, Giselle," said Copernicus. The weak gnome lay powerless to soothe his fiery servant.

Darla, I don't think that's wise. Give me control.

Darla readied to eject herself. *We do this together, right?*

Dylan nodded.

And you'll protect me, right? she asked.

"With every ounce of my body."

Giselle stared at him, disgusted and confused. Meanwhile, Copernicus breathed heavily.

Together, they began to heal him. Darla exited the other eye socket, shutting out Dylan's light but for a moment.

23

Giselle screamed and leapt back, while Copernicus lay blind and paralyzed, unaware of what was happening.

Dylan dropped to one knee.

Darla probed the elder gnome's functions and unknotted the poison from pressure points. After a moment, Copernicus breathed well again.

Giselle was near to hyperventilating as she reached for the nearby broom. Dylan stood to meet her.

"Guards! Police!" she cried. "Anyone! Help, please."

Giselle sideswiped him, and Dylan caught her backswing. The two tugged on the broom as Dylan bled from Darla's exit passage.

Darla's suckers clip-clopped in dark magic like an excited corn popper, weaving her spell. Dylan's suspicions proved correct. This poison was unique and deadly.

Adventure surged through her veins as she unclogged the gnome's own channels. The man's thyroid swelled, and Darla kneaded the lump, working her eldritch powers.

Dylan turned Giselle around, and she checked her shoulder at her master.

"Get away from him," she cried.

Giselle released the broom only for Dylan to tackle her.

"She's healing him," he growled.

His worn arms swelled, tossing her back. He shielded Darla as Giselle rolled for the broom.

"Finish!" Dylan barked at Darla.

Darla's suckers clacked in a clap of thunder, relinquishing the final blow. Copernicus broke wind, and the gnome shot up.

Giselle swatted Dylan until Copernicus lurched. The gnome fell forward, and Darla raced to Dylan's ankles. Immediately, Dylan scooped her up to safety, and together they reveled in the great deed they'd accomplished.

His color returning, Copernicus faced his servant. "Giselle?"

The crane pushed Dylan aside and enveloped her master.

Dylan dusted himself off, and Darla perched upon his shoulder with a smirk. Adventure throbbed in her suckers, finding excitement out of her skull. Literally. This was what she'd been waiting for all day.

Giselle turned to them astonished, and Dylan pulled up his cloak before the Undying Watch arrived. He exited the tent into the twinkling stars above. He hurried his step, but Giselle followed.

"Wait," she cried.

Dylan stopped.

"Who are you?"

The street rang with the clanking of police metal. It was the bazaar police! Dylan bolted to the safety of their sleeping alley. He didn't bother stopping until he knew they were safe.

Alone in the dark, Dylan slid his back against the wall, and Darla beamed at him. She felt his weakness growing, this time much like the others, so Darla drummed her magic to repair his wounds. Dylan cupped her against his chest as the wind tossed brisk chills between them. Darla kissed his palm. It would be another hard, icy night like many others.

Dylan's "little wish" spoke to him as his eyelids grew heavy. "Do you think we got the job?" she asked.

"Let's hope, dear. Let's hope."

"You think they'll give us new clothes? I'd adore us some new socks, Daddy."

Dylan yawned. "Maybe. We'll beg them for food tomorrow. You did well, dear."

Darla beamed.

Wrapping his cloak, her host shivered, frail and cold, in the alley. No bed. No warmth as he shut his eyes. If they were lucky, his stiff motor functions wouldn't need a jumpstart in the thaw of daybreak.

Darla's host had swapped bodies three times before the age of thirty, and that wasn't the worst part.

The worst was that she was stuck with him. Nothing and certainly not Darla could stop their next swap, and it was all her fault.

Sometime between swaps, she had eaten the location of Dylan's original body from his brain and searched for remnants of it ever since. Her mother had been right in that they were destined for greatness, but not like this.

They needed the *real* Dylan, and she could feel it.

What was worse, Darla couldn't help but feel responsible somehow, even though the body's loss had come by accident.

Luckily, the taste had left one small clue, lost, buried and succulent. It hinted sweet, something burning, something buried, something—childhood.

She recalled a girl who held the stars, as cryptic as it was. Her lashes fanned, familiar yet distinct. A name danced on the tip of Darla's tastebuds, but in the end it eluded her. Who was she?

Darla resigned herself to nuzzling closer to Dylan. No matter what, she would fix this too.

For better or worse, all they had was each other. Without each other they meant nothing—and she preferred it that way.

Shivering, Darla burrowed beneath his clothes for warmth. She'd watch for burglars and troubling signs while he slept. Perhaps she'd dress up her daddy warm soon. That much would change. Tomorrow, a new life and a new body lingered, ripe for the taking. She could feel it in her tentacles.

Until then, his wool socks would keep her warm.

Darla's eye blinked lazily, and she fought back a yawn.

Trumpeting hoots of skunk-owls, otherwise known as

scowls, broke through the night, making Darla jump. The birds took flight, dashing across the bed of stars and twinkling city lights.

Darla gripped the edge of the elastic and burrowed, looking up. Now wide awake, she scowled back at them.

Darla would be happy if she never saw another bird in her life. Especially Giselle.

Darla's eye widened. That was it! Giselle—she was the girl from the memory. *She held the bracelet. She literally holds a star.* Darla had to wake Dylan. Maybe if they hurried . . .

Dylan snored, and Darla stopped to smile.

It was no use.

Darla kissed her daddy goodnight, and as she gazed at the stars, she felt the worst of it was over. Tomorrow, their luck would change.

Darla had swapped bodies three times before her host aged thirty, and the best was yet to come.

THE END

THANK YOU FOR READING

*T*HANK YOU FOR READING!
If you enjoyed please be sure to leave a review as this helps others discover if this book is right for them and goes an incredibly long way. It can even be as simple as what you liked and didn't like.

ALSO IF YOUR want two more free short stories and updates on what's coming next, please sign up using the link below.
https://theantonioroberts.com/newsletter/

ALSO BY ANTONIO ROBERTS

STANDALONES

Lafonda and Leo Heroes of the Land

THE VESTIGE SAGA

Book One: *Vestige Rise of the pureblood*

Book Two: *Vestige What Lies Beneath*

COMING SOON

The Hollow Death of Belladonna Bates

NEWSLETTER

Do you want more stories like this?

Sign up to the Mustache Cartel Newsletter below for updates and two free short stories!

https://theantonioroberts.com/newsletter/

ABOUT THE AUTHOR

Antonio Roberts lives in northern Virginia with his family and most of his life has had a strong fascination with stories.

While not writing fantasy or science fiction, he enjoys volunteering at his local church, playing guitar, and game mastering tabletop roleplaying games.

facebook.com/AuthorAntonioRoberts

tiktok.com/@mustache_cartel

amazon.com/Antonio-Roberts/e/B08684LJMG

Made in the USA
Middletown, DE
28 April 2023

29237364R00022